Ana & Andrew

Summer in Savannah

by Christine Platt
illustrated by Sharon Sordo

Calico Kid
An Imprint of Magic W
abdobooks.com

About the Author
Christine A. Platt is a historian and author of African and African-American fiction and fantasy. Christine enjoys writing stories for people of all ages. She currently serves as the Managing Director of The Antiracist Research and Policy Center at American University.

For Granny, Grandpa and the Palmer grandchildren. —CP

For My sister, My best friend and the funniest woman I know. —SS

abdobooks.com

Published by Magic Wagon, a division of ABDO, PO Box 398166, Minneapolis, Minnesota 55439.

Printed in the United States of America, North Mankato, Minnesota.
102018
012019

Written by Christine Platt
Illustrated by Sharon Sordo
Edited by Tamara L. Britton
Art Directed by Candice Keimig

Library of Congress Control Number: 2018947941

Publisher's Cataloging-in-Publication Data

Names: Platt, Christine, author. | Sordo, Sharon, illustrator.
Title: Summer in Savannah / by Christine Platt; illustrated by Sharon Sordo.
Description: Minneapolis, Minnesota : Magic Wagon, 2019. | Series: Ana & Andrew
Summary: It's summertime! Ana & Andrew travel to visit their grandparents in Savannah, Georgia. While they are there, they learn that Grandma and Grandpa's church was built by slaves. With some help from an unusual source!
Identifiers: ISBN 9781532133541 (lib. bdg.) | ISBN 9781644942581 (pbk.) | ISBN 9781532134142 (ebook) | ISBN 9781532134449 (Read-to-me ebook)
Subjects: LCSH: Grandparents--Juvenile fiction. | Friendly visiting--Juvenile fiction. | Savannah (Ga.)--History--Juvenile fiction. | Slave system--Juvenile fiction. | African American history--Juvenile fiction.
Classification: DDC [E]--dc23

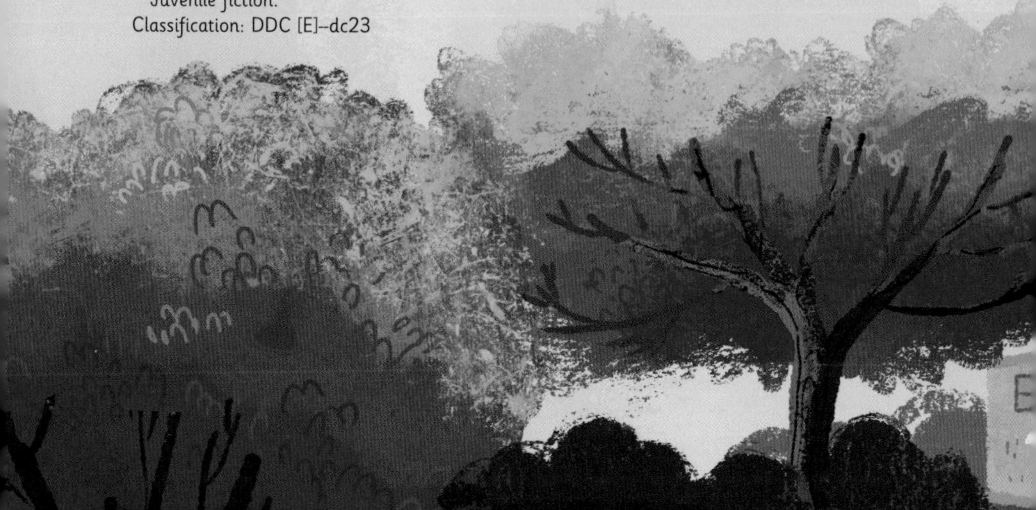

Table of Contents

Chapter #1

Up, Up, and Away

Every summer Ana and Andrew visited their grandparents in Georgia. Grandpa and Grandma lived in a little town called Savannah.

It was fun to spend time in the same house where Papa grew up as a boy. And it was one of their favorite family vacations because they took a flight to get there.

JULY
SUN MON TUE WED THURS FRI SAT
1 2 3 4 5 6 7
8 9 10 11 12 13 14
15 16 17 18 19 20 21
TRIP TO SAVANNAH!
22 23 24 25 26 27 28
30 31

"I cannot wait to go to Savannah!" Andrew did a wiggle-dance as they stood in the line at the airport.

"Me and Sissy cannot wait either." Ana and her favorite dolly sat by the window on the way to Savannah. Andrew sat by the window on their flight home to Washington, DC. They always took turns to be fair.

“I cannot wait to see my parents,” Papa said. “And I know your Grandpa and Grandma cannot wait to see you two.”

“Three!” Ana hugged Sissy. Mama had tied yellow ribbons in their hair to match their dresses. Ana and her dolly looked like sisters.

Papa laughed. “That’s right. Grandpa and Grandma look forward to seeing Sissy too.”

“Mama, what are you looking forward to on our vacation?” Andrew asked.

"I love spending time in the garden," Mama said. Grandma grew fruits and vegetables just as her family had done for generations. Andrew and Ana enjoyed helping Grandma with the harvest.

"The line is moving," Andrew said excitedly. It was time to board the airplane.

Once they were settled in their seats, Mama made sure everyone's seat belts were fastened. Ana made sure Sissy was safe in her lap before they looked out the window.

Andrew and Ana listened closely to the flight attendant's instructions. Once the airplane's engines started to turn, it moved faster and faster down the runway.

"Up, up, and away!" Andrew said. Soon they were flying among the clouds on their way to Savannah.

Chapter #2

Ahoy, Pirates!

Andrew and Ana loved their grandparents' house in Savannah. It was made of bricks and had black shutters. Last summer, Ana and Andrew helped Grandpa paint the front door red. It was very pretty.

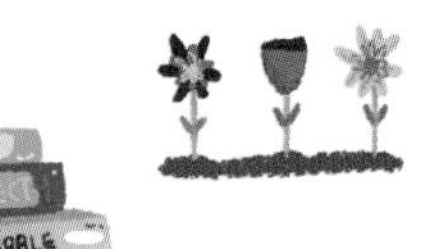

Every morning, Andrew and Ana cooked breakfast with Grandma. Then they walked with Grandpa and Papa to the library for story time. In the afternoons, they helped Grandma and Mama in the garden. Every night they played games, and Ana and Andrew won several times.

On Friday, Grandpa, Andrew, and Ana went for a walk near the Savannah River. They walked past the Pirates' House, which was one of Papa and Mama's favorite restaurants.

"Ahoy, pirates!" Andrew shouted.

Ana hugged Sissy close. “Pirates are scary. And mean.”

“Not all pirates were scary and mean,” Grandpa said.

“There are nice pirates?” Ana asked.

“There *were* nice pirates,” Grandpa explained. “Pirates haven’t lived in Savannah in a very long time.”

“I’ve never heard of pirates being nice.” Andrew had read books about pirates being adventurous. He’d even read about pirates being silly. But he’d never read about a nice pirate.

Grandpa smiled. “Let’s sit down and I’ll tell you a story. A true story.”

Chapter #3

Grandpa's Story

Grandpa, Andrew, and Ana sat on one of the benches overlooking the river. The water was calm and peaceful. Andrew tried to imagine nice pirates on their ships.

“Savannah has a lot of history,” Grandpa said. “Do you know what history is?”

Andrew raised his hand like he was in class. “Yes. History is the study of events that happened in the past.”

"And history is about people who lived in the past," Ana added. Papa often taught history to the students at his school.

"That's right," Grandpa said. "Now, for a bit of history. One of the first Black churches was built right here in Savannah."

"Really?" Ana asked.

"Yes," Grandpa said. "It was built by slaves. They built everything by hand, even the pews for members to sit in."

"That sure seems like a lot of hard work," Andrew said.

"It was hard work," Grandpa agreed. "But the slaves did it. And guess who provided some of the things they needed?"

"Who?" Ana asked.

"Pirates!" Grandpa said.

"Sometimes, pirates had extra wood from their bounties, and they knew the slaves needed it to build their church."

"That *is* nice. And pretty cool! Ahoy, pirates!" Andrew did a wiggle-dance. Ana and Grandpa laughed.

"It is cool, indeed," Grandpa said. "And I'll show you something even cooler when we go to church."

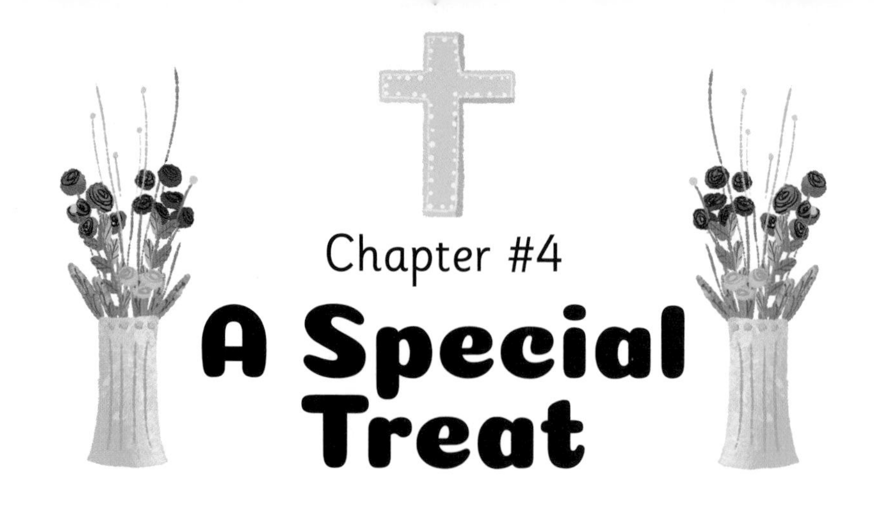

Chapter #4

A Special Treat

Grandpa and Grandma's church had stained glass windows just like Andrew and Ana's church in Washington, DC. They sat quietly in the pews. It was extra special because they knew how the pews were made. Andrew and Ana could not wait to tell their friends about the church their ancestors built.

"Did you learn about slavery in school?" Grandpa held Andrew and Ana's hands as they walked through the church.

"Yes," Andrew said. "Mama and Papa taught us about it too."

"And did you learn about the Underground Railroad?"

"Yes." Andrew remembered his teacher told him that slaves used the Underground Railroad to escape slavery.

“Guess what?” Grandpa whispered.

“What?” Ana leaned in closer.

“This church was one of the stops on the Underground Railroad.” Grandpa pointed to several small holes on the floor. “Right below us. That is where slaves hid on their way to freedom.”

“Wow,” Andrew said. “Our ancestors were very brave.”

“Indeed, they were,” Grandpa said. “Indeed.”

After church, Andrew and Ana played outside. Grandma told them to pick a few peaches to eat at the airport. Ana and Andrew picked the biggest peaches they could find.

"Dinnertime!" Grandma rang a small bell. It was the same bell she had used to call Papa to dinner when he was a boy.

Andrew and Ana ran inside. They washed their hands and sat at the dinner table. Ana was excited to see macaroni and cheese. It was her and Sissy's favorite!

After dinner, Ana and Andrew couldn't stop talking about the history of Savannah. They told Mama and Papa about nice pirates, the church their ancestors built, and the Underground Railroad. Suddenly, the oven timer dinged.

"Oh my," Grandma said. "I almost forgot about your special treat."

"A special treat?" Ana asked. "For us?"

When Grandma opened the oven door, a sweet smell filled the air. Andrew couldn't help but do a wiggle-dance. "Aye!" He knew exactly what Grandma baked for their special treat.

“Peach cobbler!” Papa shouted.

Andrew and Ana looked at each other and smiled. It was another fun summer in Savannah.